MORE PR

Because We Were

Because We Were Christian Girls is a burst of holy fire. Written with lyric heart and beautiful insight, Virgie Townsend rips open the longing heart of good girls everywhere and reveals them for all their bloody complexity. This book is a triumph of insight and imagination. Townsend's prose is both tender and excoriating, like a loving and holy spirit. The stories and the heart of this book are burned into my soul. I'll be thinking about this book for a long, long time.

—Lyz Lenz, author of *God Land* and *Belabored*

Because We Were Christian Girls is a revelatory story collection of girlhood desire for selfhood. With evocative prose and wit, Townsend portrays the harrowing world of God's love at the turn of the millennium where sparkling grape juice is a road to sin, "The internet has potential for great evil," and Britney Spears' midriff might be the Devil. Under parental oughts and steeple crosses, the girls yearn for answers that don't exist in their world. *Because We Were Christian Girls* is an urgent portrayal of fundamentalist repression of femme and queer personality through girls who to know the Spirit, must know their own.

—Crystal K, author of *Goodnight*

Because We Were Christian Girls is filled with lovely, heartfelt writing. As a collection, it will make you reconsider faith. How it can be wielded as a cruel blade, how it can feel like an infection, how its capacity can be cultivated toward self-love. Beautiful!

—Megan Giddings, author of *Lakewood*
and *The Women Could Fly*

In *Because We Were Christian Girls*, Virgie Townsend extracts beauty from a fundamentalist upbringing. Painful and darkly funny in turn, *Christian Girls* will provoke a shudder of recognition in those from strict backgrounds and foster empathy in those who are not.

—Sarah Jones, senior writer for *New York* magazine and author of the forthcoming *The Sin-Eaters*

"It's summer and Jesus loves and hates us." Honest, immersive, and captivating, these seven stories by Virgie Townsend give a candid and aching view of girlhood through the lens of fundamentalist Christian life. Townsend explores the complicated tension between the desire to belong and the need to rebel and how it feels to be "in the world, but not of it." Each story stands alone, but taken together we get an insightful and richly layered view into a culture and a family on the cusp of change. Beautifully, incisively written and deeply resonant.

—Kathy Fish, author of *Wild Life: Collected Works*

Virgie Townsend's *Because We Were Christian Girls* is a community maneuvering sexuality, independence, and faith in the stranglehold of fundamentalism. In these stories, Townsend deftly captures the energy of her characters' constant worry.

—Christopher Allen, author of *Other Household Toxins*

Because We Were Christian Girls

Because We Were Christian Girls

Virgie Townsend

BLACK LAWRENCE PRESS

Black
Lawrence
Press

www.blacklawrence.com

Executive Editor: Diane Goettel
Chapbook Editor: Kit Frick
Cover Art: "Growth" by Jamie Glisson
Cover and Book Design: Zoe Norvell

Published 2022 by Black Lawrence Press.
Printed in the United States.

For Tarlie

TABLE OF CONTENTS

CHAPTER ONE

Running

We start running when church lets out. Prayers and communion crackers are still on our lips. It's summer and Jesus loves and hates us. Or He loves us, but hates our sin. Either way, it's summer, Wednesday evening Bible study is over, and we're running out of the church building into the untended field. The grass is long and budding with feathers of golden seeds. We run with our palms out, and the grass can't decide whether to brush or scratch us.

These are the wild days. We girls grow our hair long and insouciant like horsetails. We don't think about boys. We don't dress for them or take pictures for them or worry about what they're thinking. Someday we're supposed to submit to them, but not now. For now, they're just boys. They're not God. For now, we run with them.

The church sits on a hill overlooking the highway and blue-pink-purple sky, with the steeple cross overlooking us. No one can see us. The church grounds are private. There's a house on the edge of the property, but a thicket of trees seals us off. We're in the world, but not of it. We're soldiers in the army of God, and we're children.

Our parents are running, too, but we don't know it yet. They stand in the parking lot under the lamplight talking to one another, consumed with eternity. They look like they've always looked to us: unsatisfied, unconcerned, waiting for deliverance. We don't know it yet, but the past is always at their heels. Its teeth are sharp, its mouth a void.

Nobody knows who's it or who's supposed to be hiding or who's supposed to be seeking. We keep running. We're all hiding. We're all seeking.

CHAPTER TWO

Because We Were Christian Girls

Because we were Christian girls from fundamentalist churches, we wore our dads' old, floppy T-shirts to the pool at our co-ed Christian camp. When we bobbed in the water, they puffed out around us so we looked like jellyfish with *Cancun* or *Disney World 1998* emblazoned on our chests. As we treaded water in our jellyfish hoods, we sometimes wondered aloud why the boys' section of the pool was roped off from ours—if it was just the temptations posed by our sore, new boobs, or if sperm really could swim long distances through water like my mom had told me the previous summer.

The pool's main lifeguard was also the camp's assistant pastor because it saved the camp money and God blesses good stewardship. Pastor DeMarco's blue eyes and lifeguard shepherd's crook reminded me of Dick Van Dyke in "Mary Poppins," except Bert probably never told Mary not to masturbate or that the earth is 6,000 years old.

During the day, Pastor DeMarco sat in his lifeguard's chair, surveying the gender-divided pool with a silver whistle around his neck and the crook lying across his lap. In the evening, he took to the pulpit and preached with sunscreen still glistening along his hairline.

To use the pool, we had to take a swim test when we arrived at camp. On the second day, Pastor DeMarco lined all of the campers up, girls on one side of him and boys on the other, and we had to jump in, one by one, and swim the length of the pool. As we swam, Pastor DeMarco stood on the edge, curling his toes around the cement ledge, and watched. When one swimmer reached the pool's halfway mark, Pastor DeMarco directed the next to jump in and begin.

"But if any of you jump before I say when, don't think I won't pull you out," he announced. "This is serious. I need to have my eye on you the whole time, got it?"

Pastor DeMarco was a man of God and a man of his word. My first year at camp, I hadn't yet figured out that when it was my turn, I had to wait for him to say "go" and blow the whistle. I just heard "go" and went. As I dove in, he screamed for me to stop. I hit the water before my face had a chance to turn red.

All Christian girls know what happens when they disobey, even if it's by accident. We end up pregnant, kicked out of our churches, and used as examples in sermons about what happens to disobedient Christian girls. Eventually we go to hell, where we fall for eternity in a dark, fiery pit, bound in rough chains that tear and burn our flesh, deprived of any human contact except for listening to the eternal screams of other Christian girls who are also bound, falling, and should have listened to their elders.

I thought about that as I sank to the bottom of the pool that day, and I thought about how a lot more goes into being a Christian girl than just believing in Christ, and when I hit the bottom of the pool, I thought about how long could I hold my breath. I'd never timed myself, which I regretted. I didn't want to go back to the surface. It was peaceful and blue at the bottom of the pool, and it wouldn't be up there. I waited.

Pastor DeMarco hooked me like a fish a few seconds later, catching me around the torso and pulling me back onto the pool's cement edge. I closed my eyes as I lifted myself off the ground so I wouldn't see the other campers standing in a line around the pool watching me. My dad's T-shirt clung like a tarp and dripped onto my feet. My cheeks felt warm and puffy, like two hot air balloons burning from inside and rising. I quickly pressed the shirt's baggy sleeves against my face, trying to cool down and hide my embarrassment. Pastor DeMarco leaned in to meet my gaze with his Dick Van Dyke blue eyes.

"Did I blow the whistle?" he asked.

I could have told him that I didn't know to wait for the whistle, but if you think what happens to disobedient Christian girls is bad, you should hear what happens to disobedient Christian girls who sass their pastors and parents. I didn't want him to think I was arguing with him. I looked down and shook my head.

"No sir," I said.

"What do you say to me and everyone you've made wait?"

"Sorry, sir. Sorry, everyone."

"Do you guys accept that apology?" he asked my fellow campers, but no one replied. He turned back to me.

"You go when I say 'go,' okay?"

He smiled, straightened up, and leaned against the crook like an ancient prophet with his staff.

"You can go now."

I stepped up to the ledge again.

He blew the whistle. This time I jumped, springing down on my thighs to gain momentum and then leaping with pointed toes. For a moment, I felt like I was soaring, and I prayed as hard as I could that God would transform my dad's old shirt into a sail and fly me away to Cancun, or Disney World, or anywhere else.

CHAPTER THREE

Heavenly Bodies

As the new millennium drew near, Erin's family began preparing for the apocalypse. Jesus was going to return at the stroke of midnight, appearing in the New York skyline as the ball dropped on TV and the moon turned to blood. Locusts would descend across the land while the dead emerged from their graves to prophesy among the living. The faithful would be whisked up into Paradise, their old flesh falling away as they assumed their new, glorified bodies.

Erin envisioned herself gliding through the clouds as her body shimmered into a form that was thin and incandescent. As the daughter of a pastor, she had spent all fourteen years of her life waiting for Jesus to come back. Her father, Tom, began spanking her and her six younger siblings shortly after their first birthdays, arguing that a pastor's children set the example for the rest of the church. Her mother homeschooled the children to shield them from the world's corrupting influence. Most of Erin's time was spent taking care of her brothers and sisters.

Now all of their sacrifices were going be worth it. The signs were everywhere: Wars and rumors of wars, famines, plagues, earthquakes, and the persecution of Christians. Tom read that computers wouldn't be able to change their dates from 1999 to 2000 and the world could be plunged into chaos. It was the perfect opportunity for the Antichrist to seize power and begin his seven-year reign of terror.

The Internet was new to Erin, so it was easy to believe it might disappear again. Her dad had a computer at his church office for writing sermons and responding to church members' emails. He didn't allow his family to use it.

"The Internet has potential for great evil," he said.

Erin's cousin, Stephanie, was the only teenager Erin knew who had her own email address. Erin's family visited her uncle and aunt for the holidays every year in the hopes their godly influence would persuade her father's only sibling to give his heart to Jesus. So far, it hadn't worked. Instead, on the last Christmas before the millennium, Stephanie sat Erin down in front of a plywood desk and signed her onto the World Wide Web for the first time.

"Mom and Dad say I should only use it for homework, but I mostly use it to look up music," Stephanie said.

The computer was encased in aqua blue and white plastic as if it were wearing a tropical outfit. Twinkling lights from the living room Christmas tree reflected on the screen. As Stephanie logged online, the modem screeched and buzzed like a prophet from the future.

"You've got mail," the computer announced.

Stephanie clicked the screen, tapped on the keyboard, and pictures popped up on the screen. There were boy bands wearing matching white suits and rectangular sunglasses as they posed in synchronized dance moves. Stephanie clicked again and showed Erin teenage pop starlets strolling red carpets in stiletto heels and metallic skirts with their midriffs exposed.

"She signed her record contract when she was fifteen." Stephanie pointed to one singer. "She was just like us, and now look at her."

Erin studied the singer's picture. She didn't look like she had much in common with Erin. The singer was a little older and had silky brown hair swept back by a wind machine. She wore a pink tube top ("it's pleather," Stephanie explained) and her stomach was bare and dusted with a constellation of glitter. In one hand she held a microphone; with the other she reached out toward an audience of thousands.

"She's pretty," Erin said.

"So pretty," Stephanie agreed, pulling her leg up onto the chair. "And she puts on an amazing show. What do you think that's like? All those people listening to everything you say and yelling your name? It must be so crazy. I asked my mom to sign me up for singing lessons, but she said we can't do them and ballet right now."

Last Sunday Erin had sung in front of her church for the annual Christmas pageant. Her voice was airy and sweet as she invoked the angel Gabriel appearing before Mary. Before Erin hit the carol's highest note, she'd taken a deep breath and felt a rush of air and power fill her chest.

"Maybe we could take singing classes together someday," Stephanie suggested. "We could start our own band."

"That does sound fun," Erin admitted.

Erin stared at the singer—her toned arm held out to a mass of blurred faces in the audience before her, her tongue paused on the roof of her mouth in the middle of a verse. She liked looking at her, and the feeling repulsed her.

"I don't think we should look at these anymore," she said quietly.

"Why not?"

"She's stirring up lust. That's a sin."

"Maybe they're just enjoying the show."

"That outfit," Erin said, pointing to the singer's abs, "is designed to make men feel lust."

"Okay." Stephanie shrugged and clicked out of the photo. "Sorry if I made you uncomfortable."

Erin pulled herself up from the desk, disappointed. Her parents had warned her that living for Christ meant being misunderstood, rejected, or even martyred. They had not, however, prepared her for polite disengagement. The two cousins walked down the hallway to the dining room in silence.

When Tom preached about the cost of a relationship with Christ, he typically cited his relationship with his brother Scott. They had banded together in childhood to survive their parents' abuse. Then Tom found the Lord in his mid-twenties while Scott still loosely observed the Catholic faith their family had practiced for centuries. They avoided talking about religion until their parents died. After the funerals, there was nowhere to train their anger but on one another.

Their families were preparing for dinner when Erin and Stephanie walked in. Stephanie's mother, Teri, was distributing soft-tipped utensils and coloring books at the children's table. Shannon ladled green bean casserole and mashed potatoes onto multicolored plates and handed them to the children. An electric carving knife whirred to life as Scott cut into the ham's lacquer glaze with his right hand and gripped a glass of red wine in the left. Tom shouted over the noise about the best angle to slice around the bone.

A runner embroidered with poinsettias was laid out over the table, the star-shaped blooms studding the hem. A floral basket of frosted pinecones and peppermint carnations sat in the center. Red scented candles burned at each end of the table. Erin smelled their sharp spiciness mingling with the ham and mashed potatoes. Two places were set next to each other in the middle of the table with a clear, sparkling liquid in plastic champagne flutes.

"Surprise! Mom said we can sit at the grown-ups' table this year," Stephanie exclaimed, holding out her hands at the display. "She said she'll watch the little kids so you and your mom can relax. What do you think?"

"Is that real champagne?" Erin asked. She would have been shocked if her aunt and uncle served alcohol to teenagers, but one couldn't be sure when it came to the unsaved.

"No, it's just sparkling grape juice, but it's still very sophisticated."

Stephanie pulled out her chair and sat down with a ballerina's lightness, her face tilted up in a prim, self-satisfied expression. Erin tried to emulate her cousin's graceful gestures, but felt stiff and awkward in her body. She was conscious of her mother standing next to her, trying to maneuver Erin's wriggly baby sister into a highchair.

"Look, Mom," Erin said. "Sparkling grape juice."

Shannon glanced at Erin's glass, and Erin spotted an instantaneous tic in the corner of her mouth.

"Yes, I saw that," she replied, turning back to the baby.

Erin added "sparkling grape juice" to her mental list of things to avoid, just another item thrown on the pile.

Scott tapped his wineglass with a spoon.

"We're fortunate to have a pastor in the family, so it's only right that he say grace before we begin," he announced, smiling at his brother.

"They're getting along," Erin whispered to Stephanie.

"For now."

Erin's father took her uncle's place in front of the room. Everyone closed their eyes and bowed their heads. This was a moment Erin loved— the communion of silence and shared belief.

Tom thanked the Lord for becoming the baby in a manager more than two thousand years ago so that mankind might have eternal life. He prayed that their hearts would be soft to hearing God's word. He praised God for the many blessings He had poured out over their lives.

When he said "amen," the rest of the room echoed him. Out of the corner of her eye, Erin saw Stephanie cross herself. She liked watching the movement. It looked soothing to lightly touch one's chest and think about salvation.

"Try the sparkling grape juice," Stephanie said eagerly.

"No, thanks."

Stephanie shrugged, pinched the plastic flute between her thumb and forefinger, and took a sip.

"This is how they drink it in Paris."

"Very fancy, ladies," her aunt Teri said with a wink.

It occurred to Erin that elegance might be a quality a person could practice and learn, not one that she had to be born with. Stephanie could transform at will into a dancer, elongating her torso, lightening her arms, and softening her hands. She could choose to move her body to please herself.

Erin mostly thought about her body when she shopped for loose-fitting shirts to minimize the appearance of her breasts, which she prayed wouldn't get any bigger, or when she ate little slips of fresh white paper between meals to try to quiet her rumbling stomach. She hadn't thought about how she wanted to present herself—whether she was charismatic like the singer, or refined like Stephanie, or mysterious, or athletic, or funny. Those felt like questions she wasn't allowed to answer in a world on the brink of ending.

The sound of happy chaos began to lift Erin and carry her away. Tom and Scott argued about a football game with dramatic boos and exclamations of "you're kidding me." Teri crouched down at the kids' table, puckered her lips, and flapped her arms as though they were short, oscillating fins. The baby smacked her palms on the highchair tray and squealed in delight at the noise she made. Shannon called over her shoulder to tell Erin's younger siblings to eat their green beans.

"So, what else do you know about that singer?" Erin asked Stephanie as she cut her ham into small pieces.

"Which one?"

"The one in the belly shirt."

Stephanie described the fated love between the singer and a fellow pop star, her virginity, her small Southern hometown. Erin pushed candied yams around her plate, shaping them into a smaller-looking pile, and listened intently. Here were clues about the kind of girl she might have been with different parents.

"We can listen to her album after dinner. I'll show you some of the choreography."

Shannon shifted in her chair and Erin's heart quickened, worried her mother had heard Stephanie's plan. But Shannon was looking toward the end of the table at the brothers.

"Jesus, can we have one holiday where you don't try to convert me?" Scott said.

Stephanie gave Erin a knowing look and rolled her eyes. Their family gatherings often began with the brothers exchanging updates about work, their children's activities, and home improvement projects. After they relaxed into the meal and old patterns, they ventured into more dangerous topics: who received less affection from their parents in childhood, who knew more about a given subject, and ultimately, which of them would or should go to hell.

"I'm just saying you should get your heart and your house in order for when Christ returns," Tom replied. "I'm worried about you, Scott. You're drinking again."

He exuded a studied calm, but Erin saw a slight tremble in his hand as he held his fork. She could sense his nerves crackling under the skin. With a gentle solidity, Teri placed her hand over her husband's and Erin understood that it was a message between them. Everyone waited for what they knew was coming.

Scott smirked and took a long drink. His wine glass caught the overhead light, and its color reminded Erin of crushed velvet dresses. He sucked in his breath.

"Listen," he began, leaning forward. "You may have convinced a couple dozen people that you can talk to God, but I've known you your whole life. You can take that bullshit out of here."

"Jesus is coming back. All the signs are there. You're on a path to destruction and you're taking the girls with you."

"At least I don't beat the personality out of my kids like Dad did to us."

"He didn't mean that, Tom," Teri interjected.

Erin heard blood rushing in her ears. Something tight and insistent began pushing its way forward from the back of her throat. She swallowed it down. Stephanie reached under the table to squeeze Erin's hand, and Erin pulled it away.

Wasn't the obedient child the best child? Wasn't that what the Bible said parents should want from their children?

"You need to apologize, Scott," Teri said, though Erin knew it wouldn't matter.

"Don't bother," her father said, wiping his hands on his napkin and tossing it on his plate. "We're leaving."

Shannon stood up quietly and pulled the baby from the highchair. Erin slipped out of her seat and followed her parents, ushering the small troop of her siblings to the front door. The lump in her throat wanted to push forward, and questions wanted to form in her mouth, and tears wanted to come.

Her father walked out of the house without his jacket and started the car. Shannon opened the hallway closet and pulled down an armful of puffy winter coats. Teri and Stephanie followed them down the hall, their feet padding on the tile behind them.

"Please, let's just finish our meal," Teri said. "The kids have been looking forward to seeing their cousins all week."

Shannon zipped the baby's coat without looking up.

"Stephanie and Brooke are not godly influences on my children," she said.

Erin slipped her feet into her boots, took her knit hat out of her coat sleeve, and tried to think only of the feeling of the thick, scratchy fabric in her hands. Then she felt a tap on her shoulder, then the feeling of

Stephanie pulling her into a hug.

"I'm sorry about my dad," she whispered into Erin's ear.

"I'm sorry, too," Erin replied, though she wasn't sure for what.

"We'll listen to some music next time. I promise."

Erin nodded, but she doubted it.

The family drove two hours home. Erin tried to keep her siblings quiet while her father yelled to her mother about his brother. At home, he led their nightly devotions and selected the Bible passage about the fool who says in his heart that there is no God. Erin sat on the couch with her Bible in her lap and tried to take notes in her devotional notebook. Instead, she thought about the bile in her uncle's voice, and Stephanie's hug clasping around her back, and the singer's arm outstretched to the audience, pulling Erin into the sparkling filth of the world her parents had escaped.

After her family was in bed, Erin sneaked downstairs to the family radio in the living room. She turned the volume to its lowest setting and listened for two signals that her parents would soon be asleep: the sound of Shannon setting a water glass on her nightstand and her father flipping off the light switch.

The skin on Erin's neck prickled. If her parents found her listening to secular music, her father would tell her to pull her pants down to her knees and her mother would fetch a wooden spoon from the kitchen.

She waited until the house was silent and pressed the power button. It clicked on lightly as if it were a courteous bellman she had summoned. She turned the dial away from the local Christian station, past the static, until she heard bass and drums playing low. She heard a singer scaling a flight of notes on a single word—maybe the one she saw at Stephanie's house, maybe another. She took her hand away from the dial.

What would happen if she wasn't taken up in the Rapture? She might wake up on that snowy New Year's Day morning to find her parents' coffee sitting cold and black on the kitchen countertop, her younger siblings' beds unmade, and a smear of glitter twinkling on her belly. She would pick up her family's still-warm clothes from the floor, fold them, and put them away. She would call every number listed in the church directory and no one would answer. Then she would dress in something thick and warm before taking the keys from her mother's purse.

What choice would she have but to go live with her cousin? The rest of her family would be up in heaven, peeking down at her from the edge of a crystalline river—thin and sexless in their glorified bodies.

She would learn ballet and pretend to sip champagne in Paris. She would use the Internet to look at pictures of beautiful popstars in pleather. She and Stephanie would start a band.

Sitting in front of the radio in the last days of the old millennium, Erin took the pen out of her devotional notebook, held it to her lips, and pretended to sing.

CHAPTER FOUR

I Swallowed the Whale before It Could Swallow Me

I swallowed the whale before it could swallow me. It's sitting in my belly now, asleep with one eye open and watchful. When the whale is awake, it swims around in my stomach until it's aligned with my esophagus and blows white froth up into my throat. I spit out saltwater in church. When I rock my son to sleep, the whale's low song overpowers my lullaby. I know the whale is angry with me. I have upended the natural order. I don't know how to fix it.

I go to the pet store to buy plankton as a peace offering. At check out, the store clerk asks me if I keep soft corals or clams.

"They love this stuff," she says.

I don't.

"You don't have a saltwater reef tank?" she asks.

The whale headbutts my liver.

"No," I gasp.

The clerk doesn't ask any more questions. She places the nuclear green bottle in a plastic bag and tells me to have a good day.

In my car, I uncork the bottle, throw my head back, and gulp the liquid. I taste kelp rotting on a beach. A bed of coral swells in the folds of my stomach. Orange krill with transparent shells burst from eggs bobbing in my gastric acid. The whale opens its toothless mouth and breathes in.

CHAPTER FIVE

Instructions

Don't say "gay." You're not gay. You experience same-sex attraction. You can't be gay because there is no such thing. God made only men and women, designed for each other by His holy will, and any attraction that exists outside of that is sin and an aberration. The real you, the person God formed in her mother's womb, likes boys.

Don't tell your parents you have same-sex attractions. Don't tell your father, who says homosexuals are the reason God is punishing our country, or your mother, who says they could choose to be straight if they turned to God.

Avoid the new girl in youth group because that's what Jesus wants. Befriend the new girl in youth group because that's what Jesus wants. Confide in her. Push her away. Don't whisper her name when you reach between your legs in the dark. Fear that it would curl like ribbon on your tongue and unspool when you opened your mouth.

Invite her over for dinner, but tell yourself that it's just to be friendly because you're sisters in Christ. When she greets you with a hug, feel the buzz and sweetness of a hundred fuzzy-bodied bees rising up in your chest.

Watch how gingerly she takes off her shiny yellow rain boots and places them on the hallway mat like slick, tender ducklings. Observe the curved point of her widow's peak and the taper of her narrow chin, her heart-shaped face. Hear her nervous laugh as your mom asks her to excuse the messy house and how it sounds both knowing and mischievous.

At dinner, take small bites of your taco to minimize the sound of chewing the tortilla shell. Make a plan to tell her about your same-sex attractions. Deny the possibility that telling her is anything more than a confession between friends. Shake away the image of her pressing you against your bedroom wall, her lips paused over yours.

Remember you're a child of God. Remember that you could lose your church, your family, your home.

Turn to God. Don't look at the new girl from youth group. Don't ask her questions—not her favorite song, her favorite meal, or if she misses the dance classes her parents forced her to give up when they joined to your fundamentalist church.

Ignore her so thoroughly that you don't see her glancing quizzically at you. Ignore her so you don't see her shift uneasily in her chair and stop eating when your father asks her why Black people always vote for Democrats. Don't remind him that her family didn't vote before they converted because they were Jehovah's Witnesses. Don't let her know you've remembered everything about her.

When she forces out a few coughs immediately after dinner, offer her a lozenge. Leave the room when she calls her parents to say she has a sore throat and needs to go home. Listen to the door close behind her and the sound of her car rumbling over the pebble driveaway. Help your mother with the dishes. See the imprint of taupe lipstick on her leftover tortilla shell. Scrape it into the trash.

CHAPTER SIX

I Am

Three fundamental Baptist girls have a sleepover on Saturday night. They wear faux silk pajamas and sit on the bedroom floor underneath a poster of mustangs running on a beach. The window is open and the room smells of summer hay mingling with raspberry-scented body lotion. Their floral-print church dresses hang in the closet, awaiting Sunday school in the morning.

All night they've been whispering and passing notes about Jesse, the only boy in their youth group worth liking, whom they all saw shirtless at a baptism last summer, whose chest is as pale as a Coney Island hotdog, whose voice seems deeper every time they hear him pray "Father God" in church. They write in green, pink, and blue ink and hand their notes left to right, left to right with popcorn-buttered fingers.

The girls think they know all of each other's secrets. They know they all like Jesse. They all masturbate. They've shared all the secrets they have the words to speak.

The girls tie up the fronts of their faux silk pajamas to make crop tops.

They clear a path in the center of the room and create a runway. Meg finds a brown fringe leather jacket from her mother's pre-fundamentalist days and poses in front of her closet mirror with her shoulders set back and her right leg arched and flexed in front. Abby pulls a secret makeup kit from her overnight bag and dusts shimmering bronzer onto her cheeks. Shayla puts her hands on her hips, struts on the balls of her feet, and feels a power that is God or herself or both.

Fundamentalist girls are girls like any others. They long to be strong, and beautiful, and show themselves with confidence to the world.

Three girls in the church nursery in ruffle collar dresses and patent leather shoes, fighting over toys while a PA speaker carries the pastor's sermon into the room. Three girls in the church Christmas pageant wearing their mothers' bathrobes and silver tinsel halos. Three girls in Sunday school reciting memorized Bible verses in exchange for gold stars. Three girls at Christian summer camp picking up sticks from the ground after the evening service and throwing them in the fire as a symbol of their commitment to purity.

A burning bush erupts in the center of Meg's bedroom. Flames explode over the girls' heads and lick the popcorn ceiling. Branches twist out of the fire and knock Meg's books from her shelf, shatter the ceramic lamp on her nightstand, and rip the poster in half.

The girls scream, run to the bedroom door, and try to jerk it open. The doorknob melts into liquid gold brass in their hands. They yell for help, but the fire is a vacuum sealing the room shut and devouring sound.

Abby trembles and drops to the floor. She folds her body into the shape of a fist and worships, her long ponytail stretched out on the carpet.

"Not my will but yours," she chants. "Not my will but yours."

Meg and Shayla watch her in front of the flames with dazed wonderment.

The burning bush has no secrets and nothing is secret to it and before it.

How does love flow down?

It runs from God to men to women to children. Being a man is as close to being a god on earth as God allows.

Abby has two fathers, one on earth and one in heaven, and she feels love from neither. At church and home, she's told she is a daughter to be guarded, an eventual helpmeet to a man after His own heart, a future mother to more holy soldiers in His army at the End Times, and a present temptation.

It's been a month since she, Shayla, and Meg attended Christian camp together, a month since she and Jesse sneaked into the woods, he unbuttoned his khaki pants and asked her to touch it, just for a minute. "It" was the word he used, as though his penis were a separate entity from him and making its own demands through Jesse, its reluctant emissary.

She felt there was a kind of innocence in his request. His face was pleading and excited, as if they were neighborhood children and he were inviting her over to see a box of new puppies.

This must be what it feels like to drive 160 MPH in a sports car, Abby thought.

The shame came after, when Jesse pulled up his pants hastily, handed her a napkin from the mess hall, and wouldn't meet her eyes.

If any man is better than any woman, any man is better than no man for a woman. Isn't it holy to give a man what he wants?

The girls lose track of how long they crowd around the door trying to pull it open and shouting for help. Shayla feels sweat beads form over her lips, between her breasts, and down her back. She wipes her forehead and the moisture smells like perfumed oil on her fingertips. She turns from the door, stares at the burning bush, and sees its blue-heart core flickering on the Berber carpet.

"Look," she says, tugging Meg's sleeve. She points to the ceiling and the gauzy polyester canopy that hangs over Meg's bed, light and flammable as a moth's wings. "Not even singed."

"What is it?" Meg asks.

It's a questioned asked for the sake of asking, a question to begin the conversation. They all know who it is.

"What does He want?" Meg tries again.

"I don't know," Shayla says.

She knows God doesn't appear before humans without a command. He tells His followers to free His people, to name all creation, to kill their children, to spread His word. She backs into the corner of the room furthest from the burning bush and waits.

Who speaks for God?

When Shayla looks up at the church stage on Sunday, she sees a line of white men in gray and blue suits. One day Jesse will go to seminary and join them up there.

Truthfully, Shayla doesn't think about Jesse except at these sleepovers. Liking Jesse isn't about liking Jesse. It's about these notes passed between friends, this laughter among girls she's known since infancy, but after the girl who bore her.

Two souls once occupied one body, Shayla within her birth mother. Shayla knows so little about her—just that she gave birth to Shayla at a nearby hospital. There, Shayla's parents came to meet her for the first time and bring her home to whiteness—to a neighborhood, church, private Christian schools, grocery stores, ballet classes, gas stations, and shopping centers where she can go weeks without seeing another Black face.

Her friends and family tell her they don't see the color of her skin. Should she explain she sees herself? In mall stores or witnessing at the church's booth at the local fair, Shayla searches the faces of Black women passing by and wonders if each could be her mother. She considers this:

If she once lived within her birth mother's body, and her birth mother in her own mother's body, and on and on, hasn't she lived many lives as a Black woman? Won't she live many more?

Shayla used to run her thumb over the face of God in her illustrated children's Bible—blank, white, and radiating a holy rage. She wonders still about the laughter of God, a God with brown hands heavy and warm from holding humanity in Her stigmata-scarred palms.

"Maybe He wants us to just act natural," Shayla says. "Maybe we should just pretend there's nothing there."

Meg nods and whispers, "Might as well try."

They help pick up Abby off the floor and brush her hair from her eyes. Holding hands, they edge around the fire onto a bare patch of the floor and sit down in a tight circle. Meg picks up her notebook, tears out three more sheets of paper, and hands them to her friends. They all try to pretend the burning bush isn't there, even as the heat presses against them. Meg takes off her mother's leather jacket and Shayla rolls up her pajama shirt again. Abby's eyes are glassy, her mind with the fire.

"Let's play M.A.S.H.," Meg says. "I'll do you first, Abs."

She writes out M.A.S.H. in green ink at the top of a fresh page of lined paper and begins to create thousands of possible futures. In the center of the page, Meg draws a box and begins a spiral with a single point. She loops her pen around the box, a hypnotist's pinwheel.

She takes a breath and says, "Tell me when."

Where is the soul's home?

A heavenly mansion on a hill, crystalline waters streaming below and choruses of praises sounding above? The belching lake of fire? This ephemeral world? This attic room with its textured ceiling, the rose-print wallpaper, the Bible on the nightstand?

Meg feels outside her body. She thinks she has always felt this way.

She envisions a shadowy, creeping figure pulling on her skin, a dangerous energy hiding in the body of a girl.

She wakes up in the morning dreading the day and goes into the world, an interloper in her own life. She attends church, watches her homeschooling class videos, helps her mother with the younger children, but feels none of it. Even wearing her mother's leather jacket and posing in the mirror, her own face is unreal to her. Can anyone see who she truly is? Could Jesse understand if she told him?

There are rumors around the church about the adults in her life: who is struggling to overcome an addiction, whose sibling ended their own life, who's depressed and takes medication. What they lack is faith, Meg hears everyone say, what they need is to pray. Who hears the prayers of a girl who doesn't exist?

When Meg imagines where she might belong, she sees herself as a seed planted in the rich, dark earth, sleeping until a thaw.

The girls play three rounds of M.A.S.H. and no one lands on marrying Jesse. Meg deals out cards to play gin rummy. The burning bush crackles behind them. If the girls look at it too long, they become lost in waves of oranges, yellows, and blues.

"Too bad we're trapped in here," Shayla says with a growing smile. "We could get marshmallows and make smores."

"He probably wants, like, a sacrifice," says Meg. "I don't have any lambs. Do you think He'll take body lotion?"

"Stop it, guys," Abby whispers. "He can hear you."

Something begins to shake loose in the room. Meg crumples up one of their notes and tosses it over her shoulder with a joking, feigned insouciance. It disappears into the fire. Shayla gathers up her cards, tosses them in, and shouts, "52 pickup!"

"Stop it!" Abby stands up and yells at her friends and then to the fire. "Stop it, stop it, stop it!"

Close to the flames, the fire catches the hem of Abby's faux silk pajamas. Meg and Shayla watch as it runs up the inseam of her pants and engulfs her.

For the rest of their lives, Shayla, Meg, and Abby will argue about it: what the burning bush means and who holds the power to say what it means and how they'll live with it.

Who is chosen when one chooses herself?

Three fundamentalist girls walk into the fire and it holds them in peace. There is honey sweetness on their tongues and a roar in their chests. The bush's branches grow tangled ladders and trumpet-shaped blooms burst open.

The bush's branches grow a maze above their heads with three paths: one deeper in the world they've known, one beyond it, one away from it. Each girl grabs a branch above her head, bounces once, twice, three times and hoists herself onto the bough. The bush grows and burns as they climb and climb, reaching for heaven.

CHAPTER SEVEN

What Fundamentalists Do

Mom is taking me to a new church to be prayed over. Ordinarily, we're not supposed to go to non-fundamentalist churches because fundamentalists are the only true Christians. Catholics are Mary worshippers, Lutherans are half-baked Catholics, and Episcopalians are gay.

"It's a spiritual renewal service," Mom says as I climb in the passenger side of our minivan. "There's a team that lays hands on you and prays over your life. I've heard it's life-changing."

"Won't we get kicked out of our church?" I ask.

"We're just going to give it a try. We don't have to go back if it doesn't work."

The church we're visiting is charismatic. People speak in tongues and sing praise songs with electric guitars. In our church, both of these things are temptations from the Devil. Taking me to a different church means she's desperate.

Pastor called yesterday afternoon to tell her that he doesn't believe

I'm actually saved, so I'm probably going to hell. I needle my Sunday school teachers with questions. At a sleepover with the other church girls, I said maybe hell is more of a metaphor than a literal place. One girl told her mom, who called Pastor, who called my mom as soon as she got off her shift at the nursing home.

Pastor told Mom that I think I'm smarter than God. My heart is proud and defiant. He said he respects that she's a single mother trying to raise godly children in a fallen world, but it's hard when girls see their mothers working outside the home and don't have fathers to show them how to be godly women.

"I'm sorry I've got to ask you again," Mom says. "Are you sure you're saved?"

"Yes, since I was seven."

"Pastor said you also asked your Sunday school teacher why the Bible orders slaves to obey their masters. Is that true?"

"Everyone says God can handle our questions, but then they get angry when you ask them," I respond. "Shouldn't they think it's good I want to know God better?"

"It's not getting to know God better if you're nitpicking Him."

"I'm saved. I know I am."

"Okay, good," Mom says. "But you've got to stop drawing negative attention to us, Sarah. I don't want to get any more calls from Pastor about you."

"Fine."

We don't talk for the rest of the drive. I look out the window and watch the landscape shift from our Rustbelt city to rural Upstate New York. First the Brutalist architecture disappears and then everything is green but the sky and cows idling in fields along the highway.

The charismatic church is the last stop before chain farm supply stores give way to signs advertising endless land for development. When we pull up to it, I'm stunned by the church's size. It's at least five times bigger than our church—half holy temple, half concert venue.

Our church has about one hundred and fifty members. After the service starts, our deacons stand at the back of the sanctuary and count heads while the rest of us sing old hymns. Every week, they publish the previous week's attendance in the back of our church bulletin. No one talks about it, but we all know it's there. We know when the number goes up at Christmas and goes down after New Year's. We know that most of the time, it stays the same.

A greeter hands us bulletins as we walk through the double doors, and Mom and I follow a stream of people into the auditorium. The walls are painted silver-pink and dotted with frosted wall sconces that cast warm, curved light. The chairs have charcoal gray upholstery, thick seats, and arched, metal backs. There's a clearing at the front of the auditorium where a couple of rows are missing.

A professional lighting tech sits in a booth at the back of the room controlling the colors that pulse across the stage, where a five-person band plays us in. Two singers lift up their hands as they sing for God to anoint them with His blessings. They're probably only two or three years older than me—maybe nineteen—but they seem so sophisticated by comparison. One of the vocalists has on sparkling blue eye shadow that shimmers when the spotlight turns to her for a solo. She wears blue jeans and a stylish bob with blonde highlights. I'm wearing a long khaki skirt from Goodwill and am not allowed to cut my hair or wear makeup. As she sings, she's so overcome with emotion that she grips her microphone stand for support and wrinkles the space between her eyebrows like she's about to cry, like the hardest thing in her life is how much she wants Jesus.

"Right here," Mom says, directing me to a row at the front of the auditorium.

This is the closest I've come to attending a rock concert. Our church disapproves of music that isn't hymns or classical. Once when I was in

junior high, I asked Mom why I wasn't allowed to listen to Top 40 like
my classmates.

"Non-Christian music reminds me of things I did when I was young
that I don't want to remember," she said. "You won't have that problem."

She didn't say "sex and drugs," but I knew what she meant. She
believes that if she had grown up in a Christian home or gotten saved in
her teens instead of her thirties, she wouldn't have married my dad and
spent the next decade worrying about my brother and me getting into
his pain pills. She could have been one of the homeschooling, stay-at-
home moms at church who was a virgin on her wedding night and has
never had to bail her husband out of jail.

I sit down and flip through a church bulletin, trying to ignore the
sinful worship music and light show. The six-page bulletin is glossy
printed with a color picture of a burning bush on the front. It lists eight
services a week, while our church has two.

Mom stays standing and begins singing along with the worship
band. She closes her eyes, lifts up her hands, and holds out her palms
like antennae waiting to receive a divine signal.

That's when I realize she's done this before. She's been cheating on
our church with this church. She's betraying our austere, exacting God
with this wild, expressive God.

I want to puncture this church's spell over her. When the music fades
and she sits down, I shoot her a look that I hope will shame her into the
quiet, respectful piety that we observe in our church. We're fundamentalists. This isn't what we do.

Her eyes are fixed on the stage, where the pastor is walking out from
the wings. I'm relieved that he at least looks like most pastors I've known:
Male, white, and about fifty-five years old. His short hair is parted neatly
to the left. His most distinct features are his goatee and a white Oxford
shirt tucked into khakis, not the usual black or gray suit.

"I want to thank you all for being here tonight," he begins. "The

Bible says that when two or more are gathered in my name, there am I in their midst. God is in this room and He wants to pour out His blessings over you."

"Amen," Mom says.

"Tonight, our team of prayer warriors is going to meet and pray with each of you. They are blessed with the gifts of healing and prophecy." As he speaks, about thirty men line up behind him. "But before we begin, let's open with prayer.

"Father God, we thank you for bringing us once more into your house. Open our hearts to hear your words and receive your Spirit. Touch us and change us irrevocably, we ask you, dear Lord. In Jesus's name, amen."

"Amen," Mom says again.

The pastor and prayer warriors climb down the stage steps and stand in the clearing at the front of the auditorium. Mom takes my hand and says, "C'mon, we need to beat the rush."

We power walk through the crowd to the front of the room, but the pastor is already standing there with his hand on a young man's shoulder. The pastor's eyes are closed and his mouth moves in prayer. The young man wears baggy blue jeans and a white T-shirt. His dirty blond hair is shorn into a buzz cut, and there are small bulbs of purple-red acne in patches on his cheeks. A member of the prayer team stands behind him with outstretched arms. There are groups of three in similar configurations across the room.

As the pastor prays, the young man holds up his hands to the ceiling. His expression is full of questioning and hope, like he's asked someone to marry him and doesn't know the response. Suddenly, he drops. The person behind him grabs for him and lays him out on the floor like he's going to administer CPR.

The young man's mouth twitches. The pastor and prayer warrior step back. The young man lies still for a moment before jerking up like a firecracker and spinning in mid-air. He hits the floor facedown and springs up again in another spectacular convulsion.

"He's got the Spirit," Mom whispers.

The young man lies on his back and shakes all over. No one seems worried that he could be having a seizure. The pastor squeezes the catcher's arm and slaps his back encouragingly before turning to Mom and me.

"Good to see you again, Tammy," he says, shaking her hand in both of his. "This must be your daughter."

"Yes, this is my Sarah," Mom says, her voice nervous and bright. "It's her first time here."

"Welcome, Sarah," the pastor says. "Your mother told me you've been struggling with a lot of questions. God loves questions."

He smiles at me like we've just established an inside secret.

"Yes, Sarah always had a lot of questions, even as a baby," Mom says. "When she was little, she said the thing she liked most about Heaven was that we'd get to know everything."

"Inquisitiveness is a gift, but also a responsibility," the pastor tells me. "You'll have to work your whole life to bring that gift back to God. Do you want to pray together?"

"Yes, sir," I say.

Mom moves behind me, holds out her arms, and smiles. There's hope and anxiety in her expression. She wants this to work, but I'm not sure what that means. Sometimes I think she wants a different kind of daughter—the kind of daughter who lovingly trusts her elders' authority and immediately reports her peers if they say anything heretical at sleepovers.

The pastor lays his right hand on my shoulder. I close my eyes and hold out my palms.

"Dear Jesus, thank you for the gift of Sarah," he says. "Father God, you know what's in Sarah's heart. You know that she seeks to follow you, but the Devil wants to use her gifts to lead her down a path of confusion. Dear Lord, I pray that you will give her discernment to distinguish your voice...."

People are falling all around me. Some topple like dominoes into the arms of the person behind them. Others collapse where they stand so the catcher has to make a quick grab for them. Some are cackling and others cry. Many lie quietly with pained expressions of ecstasy on their faces. The floor is littered with bodies, palms out and upturned. The auditorium rings with peals of laughter, gasping sobs, and the quiet murmurs of prayers.

The pastor's prayer for me follows a formula. First, he says something nice about how smart I am, then something passive-aggressive about how that could be a problem.

"Jesus, you have given Sarah a strong mind, but pride goes before destruction, and a haughty spirit before the fall," he prays. "Touch Sarah tonight and guide her steps all the days of her life so that she will not be overcome with pride and fall into sin...."

I still imagine what it would be like to know everything in the universe. I think it would feel like being an electrical conductor: millions of atoms buzzing around inside my body as they pass through into the rest of the world.

I know why Eve ate from the Tree of the Knowledge of Good and Evil. She loved God, but she had a hungry mind. When God kicked her and Adam out of the Garden of Eden, I imagine her standing at the edge of the home she could never return to, only a little closer to all the knowledge in the universe, and alone with a man who couldn't tell her anything she didn't already know.

My arms begin to ache from holding them out. The pastor's voice begins to wear, but he continues. He and Mom are waiting for me to drop. All I have to do is fall back and lie on the ground with a dreamy smile.

"Father God, each of us is a mystery to the other," the pastor prays. "Tammy knows that she may never understand the workings of Sarah's mind, but you do, Lord Jesus. You wove her together in her mother's womb...."

Tonight, I see for the first time that Mom's looking for something.

She's a seeker and she wants me to seek with her, but we're not looking for the same thing. I think she's trying to find a church that accepts her. That's how she'll know God loves and accepts her, too, with her wild adolescence, divorce, and mouthy public school kids.

Sometimes the divide between Mom and me seems so flimsy, I understand Doubting Thomas's urge to plunge his hand into Jesus' side.

I decide to fall. I lean back on my heels and go. It feels fake and clumsy, but the air gives way around me like it doesn't know. Mom catches me with expert hands. This is what she does every day: lifting patients from their beds, setting them into wheelchairs, helping them onto exam tables, and holding them up on the way to the bathroom.

She lays me down on the floor so gently that I envy her patients. If I were a baby soul in Heaven, soft and all knowing, and God asked me who I wanted to be my mom, I'd pick her again.

I hold up my hands and relax my face. I pray my own prayer until I don't hear the pastor anymore. I pray that God will give me the hunger I need to change my life and the strength to do it. When I pray, I feel the love of God running through me like a steel beam, and I know in my proud, defiant heart that my faith is real.

There are so many things I know but can't say.

Mom's quiet on the way home. We drive down the hilly country roads in silence, back to our apartment in the city. About a mile from home, her breath catches in her chest.

"The pastor asked to talk to me after he prayed over you," she says. "He had a message about you. He said the Lord gave him a vision. You're very special to God."

"Everyone's special to God," I reply. "Every kindergartener in Sunday school knows that."

"But you're especially special to God. He said the Lord has placed a powerful call on your life. He had a vision of you standing in front of a huge crowd and a flame of truth on your head. He said you're going to be a great leader and teach people many things they don't know about Him."

Her eyes shine with gratitude, fear, or both.

"I get all the questions now," she says. "I get it."

Maybe this is her consolation for having a defiant daughter. Maybe one day I'll stand in front of a packed auditorium eight times a week and people will lift their hands when they hear my words. Maybe then our pastor and the virginal, homeschooling moms at church will have to realize they were wrong about her.

But as I lay on the church floor with my hands up and eyes closed, I saw the future, too, and felt the sorrow and freedom of a prophet—burdened by foresight, unshackled from time.

In the future, there will be transfiguration. I will leave our Rustbelt city, our church, and Mom. I'll stop wearing long skirts and start wearing jeans. I'll choose a different life from Mom's, but also different than the one she wants for me. My world will burst open and break hers apart.

I'll join secular society, but I'll always be a little fundamentalist. Just not fundamentalist enough.

Acknowledgments

In the last days of finalizing this book, my cousin Tarlise Townsend passed away at the age of thirty-one after a seven-year battle against nodular melanoma. Tarlie was a lover of the world and all its people, a scientist, polyglot, and adventurer. There is much she's given the world, and still much more we'll continue to learn from her bold and generous life.

After writing a book about salvation and damnation, I know only that love is eternal. I've loved you since before I can remember, Tar, and always will.

I believe. I believe I'll see you again.

Every book arises from a community of believers. Many thanks to the editors who first believed in these stories. They include Nate Tower at *Bartleby Snopes* for publishing the titular short story; Christopher James of *Jellyfish Review*, which featured "I Swallowed the Whale before It Could Swallow Me;" Kim Magowan from *Pithead Chapel*, who pulled a much rougher draft of "What Fundamentalists Do" from the slush pile and refined it; and Thomas Ross at *Tin House* for beautifully editing and publishing "Running."

Black Lawrence Press was my first-choice publication for this chapbook. Thank you to Kit Frick, Lisa Fay Coutley, Diane Goettel, Zoe Norvell, and the BLP team for making this dream come true and creating a nurturing publication process.

I am indebted to flash fiction maestro Kathy Fish, in whose workshop I wrote "Running;" the incredible sensitivity reader Phoenix Lotus; Hillary Leftwich for her brilliant edits on "Heavenly Bodies;" and the *SmokeLong Quarterly* crew.

To write about Christian fundamentalism, it was important to reexamine my own upbringing and strive to better understand and honor other people's experiences with the movement. I'm grateful to the Facebook group of independent fundamental Baptist survivors, with whom I've found fellowship. I'm also appreciative for the deep research and insights of *The Child Catchers: Rescue, Trafficking, and the New Gospel of Adoption* by Kathryn Joyce, as well as transracial adoption writer and educator Hannah Matthews.

The cover art was created by Jamie Glisson, who was there the day I was pulled from the Christian camp pool—the incident that inspired the "Because We Were Christian Girls" short story. She was there again when it was time to design a cover that speaks to the heart of these stories and to many people's experiences.

And finally, my love and gratitude to my parents Kim and John, siblings Lula, Lisa, Rebecca, Lorraine, and Johnny, and most of all, Ryan and our children. Thank you, my honey, for reading each of these stories countless times and acting as their greatest evangelist.

© Bridget Florack

VIRGIE TOWNSEND (she/they) is the author of the fiction chapbook *Because We Were Christian Girls* (Black Lawrence Press, 2022). As a fiction writer, essayist, and reporter, her work has been featured in *The New York Times, Tin House Online, Washington Post, Harper's Bazaar, VICE, SmokeLong Quarterly,* and *Jellyfish Review,* among other publications. Virgie lives in Syracuse, New York, with her family. Find her online at virgietownsend.com.